Idlegain: A Novella

Idlegain: A Novella

Mattie J. Garby

HGREENBARGEDGYPRESS

Printed in the United States of America

First Printing, 2018

ISBN 978-1-7325029-0-1

Contents

For my family who has always supported me.

And for David, you are my fountain of inspiration.

Cover photo by Mattie J. Garby

Author photo by Mattie J. Garby

Author's Note

This book is part script, part novel. If you want ten pages of a commentary on a rose garden or a cup of tea this is not the book for you.

If you like short sentences and taut dialogue then you've come to the right book.

Be warned. There is strong language in this book. This is the real world and this book is not intended for children.

Enjoy the ride,

Mattie J. Garby

1.

Downfall

Convenience is our downfall.

Year 2030

"Video rental," I read out loud.

The brick and mortar stores are mostly detonated. Piles of blocky computers and video game consoles have long since smoldered after a well-timed raid and roast. I take the long slogs in the sewers and vault my way across fire escapes and construction sites. If I was seen by any government agent or detected on a machine's radar I would be a dead man. My kind, the kind of person who lives by old-fashioned hunt-n-gather rules, is a pain in the ass to the Idlegain society. Peace would be achieved they said. No one has to die they said. Technology would rule the world. And it did. Until the blackout.

I crouched in the doorway holding my mom's Glock in front of me. "Anyone here? Hello?"

The truth about society went over most people's heads. No matter what we built or thought we had achieved, no matter the benefit of advanced technologies, it was all doomed to fail. The films were wrong. Media culture brainwashed almost everyone. Realistic expectations were forfeited for the dream of a self-made utopia on Earth. There is no utopia. I can attest to that. My name's Ryan David and I'm thirty-nine years old. I stocked shelves before going on the run from the government.

"Hello?"

I pointed the gun at the main store counter. Something moved behind it. My fingers tensed.

"Don't shoot!" A young woman popped up shielding her face with her hands. "I'm a Relic like you."

"Prove it," I said.

"I don't have the implant. You can search me."

I wanted to trust her. She was cute. Her outfit was nothing like the sleek mandated uniform of the era. She wore plaid flannel, blue jeans, and laced-up hiking boots. Country girl with long auburn hair in a braid. Reminded me of my grandmom. I come from a mountain family and the women in my line don't put up with bull. I had to speak careful.

"I'm Ryan."

"Norah."

"How long you been hiding here?"

"Down there." She pointed to the floor.

I lowered my gun, stepping closer. "What you talking about?"

"I hide them down there."

"Hide who?"

Norah bent down and slid her fingers under a latch bolted to the floor. She pulled upward, revealing a secret door and shallow room beneath our feet.

"Maguro. Sakura. My babies." She gave a curt whistle and two full-grown Siberian huskies appeared at the bottom of the shelter.

"Well." I secured the gun at my hip. "Ain't that easy carry-on."

I followed her down the makeshift ladder. "Care to explain why you got two dogs with you in a video store?"

"Had no choice. Intellects almost cornered me. Found a sledgehammer and did some construction work." She waved an arm around. "My secret spot."

"So how long you been here?"

"In this place? Four days. Then a man like you sniffs me out. Damn Intellects will catch up soon."

"I'm not on their side, dear. I swear it."

"Don't call me that." She knelt down and dug through a ragged cardboard box filled with blank VHS tapes. Her sleeve rode up her arm, showing a bulky tactical watch strapped to her wrist.

"Listen," I said. "I think you should come with me."

"No."

"I know where you'll be safer. The dogs too."

The hair in her braid began falling around her pale cheeks. "You don't know enough."

"You refused the implant."

"I did." Norah sat back on her heels. "I paid for it."

"You can't stay here. They're tracking us. Tracking me."

"I have no idea who you are, Ryan. The only reason I let you in is because I knew you were a Relic."

I shrugged. "Where's the proof I am?"

She gestured to my holster. "Gun."

"Oh." I smiled, glancing down at it.

"Only Relics carry them. Usually in secret."

"I'm sorry I scared you." I dropped to one knee. "I haven't felt safe in months. Didn't expect to see a pretty girl in flannel in a ghosted video store of all places. And your dogs seem very sweet. What were their names?"

Norah's smile had dimples. "Maguro and Sakura."

I nodded. "Japanese."

"Yes."

"I had a cat named Yoshiro. He was a jumper. Sailed over everything. Even the fridge."

She continued to smile as I talked. It was surreal to have a normal conversation. I hadn't spoken directly to a person in weeks. Kind of like a first date at the end of the world.

"Do you know your way out of the city?" I asked her.

"Without being arrested, sure. But there's a price."

"What is it?"

"Gun."

2.

Forefathers

Remember the forefathers.

Within minutes of changing clothes I was ready to ditch Norah and the dogs, but the girl knew rules I did not. The Glock was buried and the key was in my boxers. I hated taking orders.

"So this is what daylight looks like."

"Never been in public?"

We walked shoulder to shoulder, each holding a leash. The uniforms were too tight and far from sweat-proof. Blending in was the only way. Miserable as hell.

"Not in the middle of so many sheep," I said.

Our current society resembled a mash-up of a modern doomsday film and a giant arthropod movie from the 50s without the giant arthropods. After the blackout the only technology that existed was what the government handed out. It was a device used for all purchases and citizen tracking. The gleeful advertisers called it the Idlegain.

Three years ago the commercials took over with what we Relics define as soul-sucking propaganda. The majority of the population volunteered without reading the fine print. The rebellious ones who refused the implant are still being hunted. Folks like me and Norah. The commercials and billboards excitedly gab "Freedom Is Convenience" but it hides the evil faces. I had my own name for the advertisers. I called them truth-snuffers.

"Hungry?"

"No. I am not hungry."

"Granola bars in my backpack," Norah said.

"Stolen?" I asked.

"Stolen," she said.

A constant chill surrounded me as I walked with Norah, my eyes shifting from the fluffy Maguro pulling at the leash then back up at the blurred skyline. The sun was scorching but I couldn't feel it under the watch of traffic cameras and government agents.

"Dang. You are a little ninja."

Norah laughed quietly. "No. Just hungry. Help yourself, Ryan."

"Nah, I'm good. Not snacking here."

The smells on the street were delicious. Wicker chair bistros and paper napkin eateries lined the sidewalks. The big rigs mingled with the common civilians, all dressed in the same standard silk uniform in varying colors. The Idlegain implants weren't visible. Almost everyone chose to have it inserted in their arm. There were a few who had it in their ear. A microchip for humans.

"They won't arrest us," Norah said, noticing my nervous behavior. "I know this route."

"Then why," I said through gritted teeth, "Are they circling closer?"

They were scanning Idlegains. Suddenly having a fake one or none at all was a bad idea.

"Shit," Norah whispered.

One glance from an Intellect in a silver jacket to the left of us and my little granola bar ninja was off running. The guy had a tranquilizer gun strapped to his back.

"Hey!"

"Don't drop Maguro's leash," I heard Norah calling back to me.

Her voice came too late. The dog was sprinting away. Norah ran after him with Sakura. I followed her, knowing the government agent was behind me.

"Norah, get out of here!"

I imagined being shot down but felt nothing. I waited for the sting of a bullet or dart.

"On your knees! On your knees!"

Another second passed before Norah was out of my sight. I dropped on their command and saw a black leather boot rise up into my face.

I was rudely woken some time later. "What is this?"

I was being strip-searched by a slick hair man wearing a blue silk handkerchief around his wrist. He discovered the key in my boxers. The key to my Glock.

"What is this for?" he asked.

I smiled despite a throbbing eye and bloody nose.

"Stash of chocolate? Video games?" He spit within an inch of my lips. "Guns?"

I shrugged.

"Yeah. Yeah, you'll tell her. C'mon."

I was ordered to dress in a gray jumpsuit before entering the designated interrogation room. I expected psychological warfare. What I got was an attractive specimen.

3.

Plastic

Beware the plastic smile.

Her shoes looked like freshly-cut apple slices. Squeaky red from tip to heel. Her skirt was a contrasting tartar white. It squeezed her legs closed, looking plastic and thick. Her ankles and thighs were shielded by bumblebee yellow tights. My eyes locked on her shoes.

"My name is Sofie Regad."

"What's your relation to the circle of lies?"

She glanced up from her folder. "I'm a spokesperson for the Idlegain campaign."

"Ah." I nodded in mock solidarity. "The bringer of lies herself. Congratulations. It seems most of the population has jumped on board."

She sat down and uncapped a red pen. "Except a few Relics. And by the look of our records, Mr. Ryan David, you have been in hiding for at least two months." She flipped the folder open flat on the metal table between us. "You're thirty-nine years old. No job. No permanent residence. No live-in partner. And…" She paused with an evil clown smile. "No Idlegain."

I had no words to explain how much I disliked the new system in our country. I didn't think so many people would fall for the lies of the Intellects. Common men and women bought into a trap. They claimed free was better. Free equaled equality. Equality equaled happiness. So they said.

"Listen, lady. I am not the enemy here. Remember the order to ban and recycle all books? Yeah? I did just that and watched you idiots burn them down the street. So much for clean air. Or did you want an entire block of houses to inhale smoke from the burning pile of paperbacks?" I leaned across the table. "Evil woman."

Sofie seemed to snarl while keeping a composed posture. "Sit back, please, Mr. David. We're here to talk about the implant."

"I won't," I said. I crossed my arms.

The problem with "don't worry it's free" logic was that it led to a lack of quality for the masses, but no one knew until it was too late. Once an Idlegain was in the body the government had that body under their radar with every single step.

"After I show you this video you will change your mind. Lights, Dansen."

She stood up holding her jacket closed with two fingers. I watched her silhouette of curves walk by and again looked down at her shoes. They were the most beautiful part. The door slammed shut and I was alone, handcuffed to the table with a thirty inch video screen in front of my eyes. What came on the screen was all a pile of steaming propaganda crap. Instead of paying attention to the rosy drivel on the TV I daydreamed about Sofie Regad.

We were on a date at an art gallery. She asked to see me alone in the Picasso exhibit. We kissed against the wall and several paintings fell. Several very expensive paintings. I was in love with her bangs framing her face, her beautiful painted toes in red high heels. She was glowing and tossing her head back in playful girlish laughter. So sweet, so cute.

"What do you think, Mr. David?"

Sofie was back in the room, smiling genuinely at me across the table. "Isn't it amazing technology? And no cost to you."

I sorely wished this woman would jump up on the table, shriek, and tell me I had won the lottery. I'd take her to dinner.

"I hate it," I said.

"Allow me to give you some advice, Ryan. I love that name. Ryan."

Now she was schmoozing. The sly minx.

"If you can join us in indulging the law we would both sleep so much better. I'll throw in a dinner date with my secretary." She sat on the table and leaned into me. "What do you say to that, Ryan?"

"I'd rather go out with you, Sofie."

"I can arrange that. After the procedure of course."

"Of course." I smiled. "And y'all can just throw yourself off a damn cliff."

She plopped hard in her chair. "Sonofabitch." This woman reminded me of an actress for one of those irritable bowel syndrome commercials. So bent up.

"Let me go. I am not a criminal," I said.

"Today you are. You have 48 hours to report to this location."

I took the paper she ripped from her folder. "What is this?"

"You miss this appointment for the implant and we will make the choice for you." Sofie crossed one knee over the other.

"This piece of paper won't free me," I said. "Your Idlegain and your ideology is bullshit."

"I'm sorry you don't agree." She began shuffling papers on the table.

"So I can go?"

"Yes." She called in a security guard to release me from the handcuffs. "We'll see you, Mr. David."

I turned from the table, feeling her eyes on me the whole time I walked down the hall. Screw the shoes. Norah was prettier.

4.

System

Stand against the system.

The best way to stay free was by wilderness. Second best was the ocean. Without a map I had to climb skyscrapers to see what was ahead. I did this by means of fire escapes, scaling well above the surveillance cameras. By the time I saw the edge of the city my arms were sore, my knees were screaming, and I craved a bowl of mac and cheese with a beer.

A twisted metal sign reading 'Gold Heart Trailer Park' stood between me and the highway. The trailer park itself was small, room enough for fifteen mobile homes. I walked through seeing the aftermath of a recent government raid. Most of the doors were swinging open at the hinges, spaces ransacked. Piles of video games, flat screen TVs, computers burning. Books strewn all over the park grounds, pages fluttering everywhere.

I read a message scrawled on the side of one of the trailers.

-I rat her die than b part of sys tem-

Tinkly music came from inside the home. I went in to survey the interior. Photo albums were stacked on the little kitchen table. A purple music box still trying to play had been smashed on the floor. Crimson footprints and hand prints, large and small, covered the hallway. I walked to the master bedroom. A large cedar chest opened on the bed. Weapons had been taken.

"Relics," I whispered.

I exited the trailer to hear angry shouts coming from all sides. I dropped to my stomach and army-crawled under the trailer. Grass was overgrown underneath. Dead rats, skittering spiders. I was perfectly hidden.

"Come out! Line 'em up! Out now!"

"Drop the gun! Drop it!"

"Chad Wagley, you and your family are overdue for the Idlegain."

"Put the gun down!"

Adjacent to my hideout was a family being forced out of their home. There was a dad, mom, and it looked like three kids. I saw several government agents taking position around them.

"Chad Wagley, put the gun down."

I kept hearing talk of a gun but did not see one. The family didn't seem to resist being led to the dark blue van parked on the ragged grass. I heard nothing from the kids as they were taken from their home.

"Mr. Wagley, we promise you will have everything you need. A three bedroom house, groceries, great school for the children. Come with us. Come with your family."

A long silence followed. A sudden downpour startled everybody into glancing up at the sky. Then there was a scream.

"Chad!"

It came from the mom. Through the blades of grass I could only see their legs.

"Chad!" Her voice cracked.

There was a single gunshot. The dad of the kids buckled to the ground. Dead. I covered my mouth as soon as the kids started crying. I closed my eyes and pressed my face to the wet grass.

5.

Commodity

In the words of my grandmom, "Freedom is a commodity, honey. It's an illusion we buy and sell."

When I was thirteen years old I saw a funeral procession for a fallen soldier. He was hailed as a small town superhero. I remember watching them carry the flag-covered casket and thinking heroes are expendable. Heroes are cheap commodities. One death means nothing to an empire of frauds and money gilders.

I sobbed.

"Ryan? What are you doing?"

I saw a pair of musty brown hiking boots with white bandannas tied around each of them.

Norah?

Something furry pushed up against me under the trailer. I turned my head to be licked on the nose. Siberian husky.

"Norah," I mumbled. "Norah, where'd you go?"

"Right here."

I slid forward from under the trailer. "Tell me you didn't see what I saw."

"Suicide? Yeah. Saw it. You need to eat something." She held out a stale bagel.

"I can't. Not in front of the dead."

"They took his body. No witnesses here," she said with a smirk.

I frowned.

Norah lifted her arms up. "Do you see where we are?" She pointed to the city behind us. "Do you see where we came from? They don't give a shit what happens to us." She knelt down to pet both her dogs who were singing for attention. "This is life right now. I saw people take their own lives for days at a time. Where were you?"

I rubbed my hands up and down my clothes. I was still wearing the jumpsuit that had been forced on me.

"Change out of that crap." Norah unzipped her backpack and threw a t-shirt and shorts at me. "The beach is just across the freeway."

I looked at the spot in the grass where the man had died from the gunshot. Traces of blood. No gun.

"Tiger." Norah patted my arm. "You and me. Let's go."

Her smile was a comfort. I didn't know if she was late teens or early twenties but the girl had guts.

"How'd you find me?"

"My dogs led me back. But I thought you would take their offer."

"I'm a Relic. I had a gun on me until you took it. Why would I throw away my freedom just like that?"

"You never saw the outside. You were hiding underground when they took my family and everyone else. I saw things and I know things you don't."

"I know who they are."

"Would you choose life with an Idlegain over suicide?"

"I don't know. I'm not there yet."

Norah turned her back to me. I wondered what else she was carrying in her backpack. She had clothes, snacks, dog treats. All stolen I was sure.

"We can get past the security if we leave by car," she said. " They only scan people on the street."

"And how are we supposed to get a car?"

"Trust me. I know a guy."

The guy Norah had in mind was a renegade civilian. Name was Earl Quikly. He was one of the good guys employed by the government with access to a taxi, luxury studio apartment, and a top salary. Norah refused to tell me how they met, but according to her he was our ticket to freedom. He had a defective Idlegain.

"So," I said. "How do we make contact?"

"He drives this stretch of road the same time every day. I know his car and I'll flag him down."

Our society had changed in a way that there was no longer such a thing as bumper to bumper traffic. Each citizen was only allowed a certain driving period per month, and that of course was kept track by use of the implant. The Intellects and their ingenious plan to save the world included less pollution and less road rage and that meant controlling who owned vehicles and how often they got to operate them. We could only travel so far without one and they knew it. Families were assigned housing within the city limits so they were near the government-supplied supermarkets and work sites. All of this meant for very sparse highways.

The flaw in Norah's plan was all too obvious. The last thing I wanted to do was run onto an open highway with aircraft cameras circling above us. I was being watched by Sofie Regad and her merry men.

"We've got 48 hours, Norah."

She had strapped on her backpack and wound both dog leashes around her wrists before swinging a leg over the guardrail.

"Before what?"

"Before those bastards come for us."

6.

Childhood

Don't forget your childhood.

A summer fragrance of charcoal, hot dogs, and cigarette butts. That's what the ocean blue reminded me. Being a kid outdoors, swashbuckling with friends, the family car smelling of sunscreen and potato chips. The seats sticky with melted chocolate and the munching of stale pretzels. Rolling down the windows to let a fart out.

My generation had a childhood of dirt clod wars, line tag, and daily competitions during recess. Weekends meant video games and those darn computer math games for the smarty-pants. Who could jump higher on the trampoline. Pool parties with the parents barbecuing and the munchkins cheating at Red Light Green Light.

I was lost in a memory and halfway across the four lane freeway when a cacophony of sirens swooped in. Norah stopped fast, her boots scuffing the asphalt. Her head swerved one way then flung to the other. I thought it before she yelled.

"Shit!"

She sprinted with her dogs, small legs taking massive bounds toward the beach. In the minutes I spent daydreaming I completely missed the fact that there was no simple path to the sand. What came on the other side of the guard rail was a cliff. It looked like a sheer drop from where I stood. And Norah was about to jump.

"Norah! Norah, stop!"

She disappeared over the edge. I could hear tires screeching behind me and half-expected to be shot. But there was nothing. I followed her steps to the cliff and peered over. The drop wasn't far as I imagined and Norah had a look of pure pissed-off on her sweet face.

"Get your ass down or get outta here!" she screamed at me.

I vaulted over the rail. I heard my own heartbeat in my ears as I slid to a stop. "So much for hitchhiking."

7.

Real Talk

Real talk is a lost art.

"Stay close," Norah told her huskies before unsnapping their leashes.

"This is where I'd be if a nuclear bomb hit. I'd die right here." She spread her arms and flung her head back. "I'd be gone in the glow."

"Norah, can you explain why they aren't shooting at us right now?"

"The beach is out of their jurisdiction. And the Intellects don't have the nerve to even touch a gun. It's against their agenda. They're willows."

"Willows?"

"Yeah. Willows. Easy bend, easy break. Or if you wanna say it like a five-year-old…wimpy poo-poo heads."

She sat down to take her shoes off. I reluctantly did the same. The sand was warm and fine. The stretch of beach we were on looked to only be about a mile or two, flanked by sharp cliffs. There was a pier to the right and a tunnel carved into the rock.

"Which way we going?" I asked her.

"Right. That tunnel leads to a boardwalk. No one but me knows about it because everything there is shut down."

"What's so special about it?"

Her smile was coy. "My grandpa gave me a combination. Our family safe is stowed in one of the old arcade games."

"What's in this family safe?"

"My brother's favorite hunting rifle and every written word of the government's agenda."

"And how did you get that evil manifesto?"

"My grandpa had it first." She undid her braid and her red hair fell around her shoulders. "He was part of the first wave of Relics. I wouldn't be here if it wasn't for him."

Norah's deep involvement in the rebellion mystified me. "How old are you? You can't possibly know how all this mess started."

"I'm twenty-four."

"You look sixteen."

"Very funny. That line gets old."

"You're so young. You should have been caught in the Idlegain hype years ago."

"Except I spent almost all my childhood and young adult years living off the grid. I was discouraged from smartphones, tablets, social media accounts. I only used the internet when I visited the library."

"Wow." I watched her put her feet in the ocean. "So you're a trained survivalist."

"No. What I trained for was the reality of a blackout. My grandpa knew it would happen."

"How did he know?"

She snorted. "You have too many questions, Ryan."

"Because I was underground for years just doing my job and not saying a word to anybody."

"I know because I never lied to myself about the evil." Norah grit her teeth and flung a pebble into the ocean. "You sound like you pretended it never existed. The government was just a sleeping giant right? They can't hurt you. They wouldn't dare threaten your freedom. That's what you were thinking."

"No."

"Bullshit, Ryan. You were a sheep too!"

"I am not a sheep. I didn't stand in line with a stupid smile on my face waiting for my free implant and groceries."

"You didn't do anything to stop it."

"What the hell was I supposed to do? You didn't stop them either, Norah."

"Well my grandpa tried."

"What happened to him?"

There was a long pause as Norah threw a stick for her dogs to fetch.

"Suicide."

"Was it a family suicide?"

"Almost. I ran away with Maguro and Sakura. They would've convinced me to choose a quick death over life with an Idlegain." She threw another stick.

"I don't get it. Why would they sacrifice such a beautiful daughter and granddaughter like you?"

"Freedom."

8.

Hidden

Know how to stay hidden.

The tunnel smelled like seawater and dried kelp. It was quiet except for the sound of our bare feet shuffling and the dogs panting in the dark. Walking next to such a pretty young lady was doing a number on my nerves. I began to feel like a predator being unshaven, no deodorant, and the change of clothes she gave me, shorts and baggy t-shirt, didn't help the seeping garbage in my head.

"Do you have a partner?" She had an innocent spark in her eyes as she waited for my answer.

"Ex-wife."

"Yeah? What happened?"

"It was fast. That's all."

"Was she a slut?"

I wanted to punch the wall but kept walking. "No. I was the slut."

"What?" She was laughing.

"I chased her. She lost interest two years into our marriage. Said I was boring. Why you asking? Do you have a partner, Miss Norah?"

"Nope. Never dated."

"Why not? If I was five years younger—"

"Wait." She faced me directly, pressing her chest to my body and looking hard at my eyes. "You're not that old."

"Thirty-nine."

She did the math in her head. "Okay. And I'm twenty-four. Big deal. Only fifteen years."

"Sure." I placed both my hands in the shorts pockets. "I'm not looking for anything permanent right now. I'd rather die single."

"Fine." Norah was smiling as she jogged ahead with her dogs. "The arcade is up there, see it?"

What I saw was a ramp taking us out of the tunnel and onto a deserted boardwalk. A sculpture of twisted metal that towered over the sand reminded me of a classic fair ride. I saw the remnants of ice cream stands and a music stage. There was a standalone public restroom with a little person on the door painted in a kaleidoscope of colors.

"Hey, darling, I'm gonna take a piss all right?"

Norah looked over her shoulder. "Enjoy it. It's the only thing you can do without a stupid Idlegain."

I pushed the door in and surveyed my throne. It was horrid. Puddles of urine near the sinks, skid marks inside every toilet, needles and busted drug capsules in the corners. I flashed back to the night my ex dragged me to our local bar for an hour of dirty dancing and top shelf vodka. It ended after forty minutes, Ginny vomiting in the men's room and me stumbling with her limp body in my arms all the way to the hospital. We never made it through the doors. I spewed with her.

In this seaside bathroom nothing was white. The floor was toad brown. And I was barefoot. I swallowed my vomit before backing out and whizzed in the sand.

"I didn't warn you about the public toilets."

Norah stood to my left. She was snickering.

"Thanks, dear," I said.

"It could be worse," she said. "The Intellects could have us cleaning their golden underwear."

"Wanna show me your sacred place now?"

"C'mon." She excitedly led me to the entrance of an old school boardwalk arcade. "No one knows about this."

I helped her pull the boards aside and stepped from warm sand onto cool concrete.

"No. No. No. No!"

Norah stood in the middle of the building aggressively running her hands through her hair.

"No. No. No, they couldn't. They can't. They can't do that."

Every single game, from pinball machines to motorcycle racing, was smashed.

The safe, I thought. *Where's her family safe?*

"Norah, the safe."

She dropped to her knees at my voice and scrambled through the arcade.

"It's here! Ryan, help me."

I pushed with her against one side of a pinball machine. It was beat up on top at the controls but intact everywhere else. The interior was hollow. A safe was stowed inside. A safe big enough to hold a rifle.

9.

Fear

Fear knows no creed.

Norah slumped against the arcade prize counter with the .223 bolt action rifle in her hands. Maguro laid next to her, his fluffy head perched on her knees. I flipped through the evil manifesto, a slender booklet with orange on grey words, once in awhile petting Sakura who was curled up next to me.

"Your dogs are well-behaved."

"I know."

"How long have you had them?"

"Seven years. I trained them from pups."

"I'd be awful at that. Mine would crap and pee all over the place."

Norah was stroking the rifle as if it was her lover. "I'd probably give up all this hiding and dodging if something happened to my dogs."

"Why?"

"They are the only reason I still smile."

I closed the booklet and sat forward. "Nothing in this thing speaks evil or otherwise. How can it be the official manifesto for the government?"

"Don't ask me. My grandpa just put it in there with the gun."

"Oh," I said. I tossed it aside. "It's just bullshit."

Norah nodded. "A decoy for the Intellects."

"So let me ask this then. Where were you the day of the blackout?"

She stood up, picking up the rifle with her. She began to pace. "I was here. My brother and I were playing that motorcycle game and my grandpa was trying to do that silly dance game. He was always goofy like that. Normally we would be at home on the weekends but I got everyone to come to the beach. My mom and grandma were out on the boardwalk."

"And the games shut down on you?"

"Yeah. The arcade was pitch black. No one screamed or ran. Other people around me were shaking and tapping their phones. It was more anger than fear. But then we went to the parking lot. The cars wouldn't start."

She stopped talking and looked at me for confirmation. I nodded. I remembered.

Three Years Earlier.

I was taking inventory in the stockroom. It was 7 pm. The lights went off with a faint click and there was complete silence in the store. I heard nothing from the speakers overhead and took a flashlight from my pocket to continue working. I assumed it was a temporary power outage like many other employees did. By 10 pm I clocked out and exited the store.

There was a growing commotion across the street in a well-known gated community. In the dark were uniformed men and women rounding up various individuals.

I had seen the commercials for the new Idlegain implant a few weeks prior. I knew there was a recommendation for every citizen in the country to acquire the implant but I had been told it was an option. The thought of a mandated order crossed my mind as I heard angry shouts and saw objects being thrown. I sat in my truck awhile before starting her up.

"Dammit." She wouldn't start. I tried again.

"Sir. Sir, get out of the vehicle." A police officer was tapping my window. "No one is driving tonight. Step out of the vehicle."

Shit, I thought. I unbuckled and slowly opened the door.

"Let's go." The officer motioned for me to leave my truck.

"What's going on?" I asked him as we walked through the parking lot.

"More than a damn power outage. Nothing is working. Computers, phones, public transports, satellites, anything electronic. Last news I heard was a solar flare. Could knock everything out."

"Across the street? What's all that?"

"Don't worry about it. State governor ordered all homes searched. They'll be fine."

"I live thirty minutes away. How do I get home?"

The officer gave me a rough push on the back. "Walk."

My phone wasn't working. Every streetlight was dead. Every car, in garages and on the road, was stranded. The confusion came when mobs of people flooded out of their homes and started walking in the same direction. Some still held their phones, shaking them near their ear.

"Hey man, you know what's going on?"

I looked at the kid catching up to me. He was wearing a t-shirt and plaid boxers. He had a video game controller in one hand and an empty soda bottle in the other.

"No. Do you?"

"The freaking screen went out before I could save it. You play Air Current?"

"No, I don't game."

The kid's eyes bugged out. "Damn, you're missing out."

"Where the hell are we going?"

"I dunno. They said we gotta get that Idle thing."

I stopped him with a squeeze on the shoulder. "The Idlegain?"

Families were walking by us wearing pajamas and whatever shoes they could find in the dark. They looked like passive zombies going to the guillotine.

He shrugged. "Yeah. It was on the commercial with the talking monkeys. You see it? Funny as hell."

I had seen the commercial. It was not funny as hell. It was only a cheap trick to lure the masses into buying a spectacular product. A product that boasted the ultimate convenience and freedom. The name the producers chose seemed silly to me. Idlegain. Two words smashed into one. Idle. Gain. Who the hell would think that's legitimate? And here it was. People did.

I hated change. If I had it my way we'd still be in the 90s era of technology and communication. It's not that I'm against healthy advancement for civilization, but it seemed to me like every time a new wave of inventions came off the assembly it led to more division and violence among people. The world was moving so fast that it would have to collapse one day. I was paranoid of it. And this was the night. At 10:30 pm I was walking among a crowd of sleepy and confused people toward the freeway leading into the city.

I began to slowly walk the other way. No one stopped me. I heard the sound of helicopters. Bright stick lights spotlighted all of us.

A bitchy voice sounded through a loud speaker: "Line up outside city hall. Your free implant is ready to be picked up."

Myself and a few others, including a young mother holding the hands of two toddlers, traded worried looks.

"Get your implant and wait by the freeway. We will give you a lift home."

"Your power will be resumed once you acquire the Idlegain."

I felt my insides shaking as I watched police officers surround the perimeter of the crowd. Our number was less than a hundred, just people from a normal neighborhood in a small town. I hunched before sprinting to the nearest overpass and laid on my stomach in the ragged shrubs. Power my ass. We were all dead.

10.

Rebel

Rebel is Relic.

We woke up in the dark on opposite sides of the arcade. No glow of a smartphone or tablet. Nothing to tell me where I was. I had put my sneakers back on before falling asleep and found myself sweating head to foot.

"Norah?"

I rubbed one eye and moved to sit up. My nose touched something cold. The same cold was at my back.

"Norah?"

I realized what I was feeling. I was sandwiched between two pinball machines.

"Norah, you okay? Are you here?"

"I'm here."

I tried to spot her body. Her voice sounded wobbly. I crawled in her direction, careful to avoid clunking my head.

"Where are you?"

"I'm here," she said. "Here, Ryan."

I suddenly felt smooth fingers stroking the scruff on my chin. Her green eyes sparkled in the pitch black and I relaxed.

"Thank God."

Norah smiled. "Thank you for not leaving me." She kissed me on the cheek. "This hide-and-seek shit gets old."

"It does," I said. "What time is it?"

She looked at the bulky watch still strapped to her wrist. "Damn thing's broke. Let's see what the sky looks like."

I helped her up, feeling with my sneakers that she was still barefoot and void of clothing on her legs. "Tell me you're wearing something."

"Yes. A t-shirt with cartoon fruit bats on it."

"Shit."

"Don't freak." She laughed. "I'll put on shorts. I hate sleeping in denim."

"Ditto."

It was dark outside as we walked alongside the water. I could see the beginning of the sunrise in a purple orange haze across the ocean. Norah handed me an unwrapped granola bar and in the spirit of hunger I happily bit into it. The edges of my sneakers were now damp and salt-crusted. The movement of the waves both satisfied and unnerved me. It was a deadly peace.

"How long do you stay in one place?"

"It depends." She gave me an annoyed look, flicking a piece of beef jerky in my direction. "If it weren't for you I wouldn't be on their radar at all."

I shrugged. "Sorry."

"Oh well. It was gonna happen. I've stolen so much the past month they probably have a log of it."

I watched her pour fistfuls of dried oatmeal in her mouth. She switched snacks faster than I ate them.

"Why do you bother running?" I asked her.

"Same reason you spent nights spooning sewage. Don't wanna be caught."

"Now that I see your way of travel, darling, I have to admit it's superior to mine. I never liked sleeping in the sewer, but with what was happening in the streets I felt safe."

"Then you admit to being scared?"

I looked from her green eyes to her cartoon t-shirt to the beat up cereal container in her hand. This woman was a character.

"Are Relics allowed to be scared?"

"You think I'm not?" she said. "Without my dogs I'd be a headless chicken. I don't want to run the highways alone. I hated your company at first but now…"

She touched my shoulder with her free hand and lowered my head to hers. I didn't even try to stop the kiss.

"Fifteen years, dear," I whispered, my forehead pressed to hers.

"I'm just trying to say thank you," she said.

"For what?"

"You didn't have to follow me."

"I'm not a soldier." I patted her cheek and stepped away from her. "You are."

Norah dipped her head and I could see her blushing. She gave me a quick smile before turning to Sakura who was bouncing up and down to be noticed.

"Who's so pretty, baby? Who wants lovies from mommy?" she cooed.

Suddenly I was invisible. I sat down in the dry sand and watched her romp with her four-legged lovers.

"What else do you do to pass the time?" I asked as she ran by.

"You can play with my babies too, Ryan."

"Yeah. I know." I smiled watching her red hair fly around her face. "But what about a real game?"

She gestured to the backpack near me. "I got games in there."

I rolled my eyes. "Besides solitaire."

Norah threw a stick over my head and both huskies charged past me to get it. "How do you know I play solitaire?"

"You're a woman of simple pleasures."

"Psh."

"C'mon. What game? I challenge you."

She grinned as coy as I'd ever seen. "War."

11.

Hobbies

Hobbies keep us sane.

An hour past sunrise and Norah and I were back in the cover of the arcade, shoes off, bellies half-full of jerky and dry oatmeal, seated cross-legged on the floor near the laser tag sanctum.

"Is the red natural?"

"What?"

"Your hair. Is it naturally red?"

"Yep. You playing or am I switching to solitaire?"

"I'm playing. Deal the cards."

Norah shuffled the stack of fifty-two extra fast and went about dealing them between me and her. I loved watching the concentration on her face. She looked like she was gearing up for a bloody battle.

"Your mom or dad?" I asked.

She kept dealing. "What?"

"Who had the red hair? Your mom or dad?"

"I'm German and Irish. My dad was the ginger."

I smiled. "I'm from a German background too. German and Italian."

"Hm. Blond hair and brown eyes. Okay, I see it. Let's go to war, Lieutenant Romano."

"Actually it's Lieutenant David. My last name is David."

She smirked as she arranged her cards into a perfect stack. "Ryan David. A first name as a surname. Funny."

"My middle name is Leonardo," I said.

"We playing twenty questions now? Aileen. That's mine."

"I just wanna learn about you."

"Card, Counselor Softie." She tapped the floor. "Ready?"

We flipped our cards over. I had three of diamonds. Norah had six of clubs.

"Gotcha." She snatched my card and placed both at the bottom of her stack.

"Dammit. I thought diamonds beat clubs."

"Hell no. The suits don't matter. It's the number. You never played this card game did you, Ryan?"

The smug grin on her face ignited the competitor in me. I liked to cheat in every game I played with friends, family, and my ex when we were married. It only worked with them because unlike Norah they were almost always hammered during game night. I whisked money from under a pal's nose at least once a week before the blackout and Idlegain takeover.

We flipped two new cards over. I had six of hearts. She had two of clubs.

"Gotcha," I said and put both cards under my stack.

"Nice." She started to flip another card over but halted it in the air and instead adjusted her watch. "Hang on. This thing's just an itchy piece of junk now." She unstrapped it.

"Damn, darling," I said. I gestured to her wrist where the watch had been. "Is that a tattoo?"

She glanced at the faded black ink on her inner wrist. "Yeah. It's an S."

"S for what?"

"Superhero."

We flipped our cards. Norah won the round.

"Why superhero?"

"Because I love the movies and comics. My grandpa had a decades old collection of classic comic books. Me and my brother looked at them all the time in our basement."

I won the next round and slid both cards toward me.

"I only appreciate superheroes if they grace the back of a cereal box," I said.

"A cereal box?" The tone in her voice was flat and humored at the same time.

"Yeah." I flipped another card. "I call them cereal box superheroes because of the colorful costumes that match the colorful pellets in the box."

Her eyebrows were scrunched together. "Boy, you're weird."

"I am if I told you what my other hobbies were."

She put her hands in her lap and stared at me. "Do tell."

I dramatically sighed before proceeding. "Model trains, miniature furniture, pet sitter, closet bookworm."

"What's the miniature furniture for?"

"My niece's doll house."

"What animals?"

"Dogs, cats, rats, spiders, a praying mantis."

"What books? Popcorn thrillers or the hard stuff?"

"You mean the Novocain of literature? I like Thoreau."

Norah winked and dragged her backpack over. "Let me show you something." She unzipped the front pocket and pulled out a denim-wrapped wallet. "You think you're weird. I beat you."

"What's that? Baby pictures?" I scoot over to her side, leaning my shoulder against hers.

"This was me before this hell started."

The photo in the wallet was of a red-haired teenage girl dressed like a scandalous librarian on top and a mermaid tale on the bottom. She held a fishing pole in one hand and was leaning on a homemade scepter in the other. The back of the photo read 'Halloween. 2020.'

"My gosh." I looked from the teen Norah in the photo to the one sitting next to me. "It's like you haven't aged." Her weirdness just made me smile. "You're beautiful."

I could almost feel the heat of her cheeks next to me. "Thanks."

"How did you survive all those years without social media? Where did your friends come from?"

"My family was it." She put the wallet back in the backpack pocket. "I lived off the grid. I went to a little Lutheran church set up right in the mountains and I even tried to play the organ there. A lot of quiet time like walks. I learned to hunt and fish like the boys in my family. I enjoyed it."

"You didn't ever want to leave home? Just to see what else is out there?"

"I did. But my one experience in the city…" She shook her head as she shuffled the playing cards before putting them in their box.

"What?" I asked. "What happened?"

"Let's just say it involved one of those asshole self-driving cars."

I knew what she was talking about. Convenience came with consequence. And that included the workforce.

12.

Future

Do not underestimate the future.

I quit my job the morning after the blackout. Every screen in homes, stores, and offices was down. Every car, train, plane, and bus was frozen.

I spent about an hour going through my things in my studio apartment, packing what was crucial in a sporty backpack. That same day my ex-wife knocked on my door and being a cordial party I opened it. She asked me if I wanted to go with her to get an Idlegain. The woman had no sense of a threat. For her it was just following the trend.

Three Years Earlier.

"How'd you get here, Ginny? Cars aren't working."

"I rode my bike. Look, babe. We never talk anymore but something weird is going on and I want you to come with me."

I stood barefoot in my doorway, beer in hand. "Exes don't go together. Even at the end of the world."

She whimpered, clasping her manicured hands together. "Aw. Do you think that's what's happening? Babe, please come with me. We'll find another bike. I think your neighbor chick has one."

I leaned forward and rested a hand on my ex-lover's shoulder. The top she wore barely covered her chest. "Go where? Go into damn hiding. Why you wearing a tube top? It's ugly."

"Ryan, the Idlegain. Everyone is at the city hall already. There are lines at all the clinics. I want my life back." She held up her blank smartphone. "I want this back."

I sluggishly nodded. The warm beer was getting to my stomach. "Gin, take someone else. Take your new husband."

"He already got one. He won't do anything with me unless I get it too. Please."

She was scared. I knew enough from the quivering lip and clammy hands. A painted face and flawless fashion couldn't hide genuine fear.

"Fine," I said. "Just let me finish packing. Stay out here."

The lives of modern people were dependent on online transactions and interactions. Most would do anything to get their convenience back. An implant meant access to any computer or hand-held device. It was a universal key. A universal code. A universal definition of self. It was the future.

I rode my neighbor's bike alongside Ginny. She was dressed up in one of her most expensive outfits. I never gave a shit about brand name clothes but the colors she picked always looked fantastic with her dark hair that framed her strong jaw and sultry eyes. I never considered myself an emotional wreck after the divorce, but when an ex could look like a ten on the worst day in history, that made it a hell lot harder to let go.

There were people everywhere. The city was packed with endless lines snaking in and out of public offices and private clinics. Ginny steered her bike toward a specific building next to my favorite steakhouse. She pulled up to the bicycle rack which was jammed with every kind of two-wheeler created. I hesitated, straddling mine.

"Gin, I'm not going in there with you."

"Why?" She pawed at my arm. "We get free groceries with the implant. And they have special outfits they're giving away for everybody. A top designer made them."

"I'll stick with my holey boxers and stained shirts thank you."

"It's free, Ryan. This never happens. It's free stuff."

"Okay." I gave her hand a pat. "You go in and I'll go when you come out."

Ginny rolled her eyes but said nothing more to me as she headed to the back of the line. The building was a dentist's office converted into a public assistance outpost. I noticed a lot of parents with young children and a handful of teenagers that appeared to be under the instruction of a uniformed old woman. The sour-faced school official was pacing down the line with the demeanor of a drill sergeant. The entire situation looked like a con.

I waited silently in the shade of a cafe overhang to see if Ginny would return. Two hours later she came back out. Before her eyes scanned in my direction I was running into an alley.

13.

Fight

Put up a fight.

"What did she look like?" Norah asked.

"Glazed eyes, stiff walk. She was dressed like an Intellect."

"How did you know she was an Intellect?"

"I didn't know about the Intellects until a few months later. Suddenly I was being chased by the government for breaking the law. Idlegain was the law." I looked into her eyes. "And my ex became a part of it right there and then. Not a day later and I was sleeping with one eye open in the city's sewers. The gun you made me give up in the video store…that was all I had on me."

"What happened to your backpack?"

"Too many memories. Left it in the sewer. I just wanted to hide and pretend like none of it was happening. I heard the arrests. The riots. The resistance up there. I heard it. But I never wanted to look."

We were kneeling across from each other during our chat when angry voices came from outside the arcade. Norah looked to her right at the rifle on the floor. I ducked behind a race car game. "Norah, forget the gun. Leave it."

"Stay down," she growled at me. She picked it up and stood in the corner of the laser tag room.

I closed my eyes and kept my head down. There was a gunshot. A scream and a thud. A stream of cussing followed.

"Asshole," I heard Norah say.

I opened my eyes. It was one man come to extract us. He was unarmed. Norah and I approached, examining his injury. She had shot him in the crotch.

I loved a woman who could shoot and she was girlfriend material right there and then. "Attagirl," I whispered. Taut legs, little muscled shoulders, ample chest. Damn.

"Come out. Out now!"

"Norah Dean, Ryan David, you are overdue for the Idlegain."

We traded looks. The man on the ground was a scout. Sofie Regad came into the arcade flanked by two male agents. She side-eyed the rifle.

"Get out," Norah said. Her voice was shaking.

"You won't shoot me." Sofie smiled in my direction.

"No?"

"Your dogs. Do you hear them?"

"They're outside." Norah listened to the distraught howling and barking and her grip on the rifle loosened.

"My men have them." Sofie stepped forward. "You are under arrest."

"My dogs," Norah said. I could feel the mom instinct flare in her voice.

"Cadd, Drew, take Miss Dean and Mr. David to the van."

"Give me my dogs."

"Let's go." Sofie took the rifle from Norah's limp fingers.

I allowed myself to be led outside, unprepared for the scene at the beach. Three other agents were wrangling Maguro and Sakura into a separate truck. The huskies were making mournful woo-wooing sounds.

"You bitch! Give me my dogs!"

Norah ran toward the truck with two agents dragging her backward. Sweat and tears clung to her hair and face as she fought against them.

"They're mine! They're my dogs, you ass!"

Her guttural screaming broke when Sofie ordered the truck closed up with the dogs inside.

"You bitch! I want my dogs! They're my babies! I'll kill you! I swear I'll kill you if you don't let them go!"

I was scared shitless. Norah had lost her mind.

"Get them in the van now," Sofie ordered.

Norah's anger turned into childlike wailing as we were pushed into the back of a van. I sat in the corner furthest from her as she wore herself out crying. My knees were pulled up to my chest and my head against the boarded interior. It felt like we were on our way to a real prison with barred windows and metal toilets.

We both were in handcuffs. We were sweaty, barefoot, and looked a bit like hungover beach bums. I looked at Norah who had quieted to shoulder-shaking sobs. She met my eyes. Hers were red.

"What you looking at?" Her voice sounded like a demon had invaded her vocal cords.

I mouthed to her before speaking.

"What?" she grumbled and pressed her head against the wall.

"They'll be okay."

"No, they won't."

"They'll be okay," I repeated. "Norah." I chose to stay in my corner. "Norah, it'll be okay."

"No. Not until I make that bitch pay."

"Okay."

"Bitch," she said again.

"Sh." I crawled toward her. "Let's not antagonize. Relax. Take breaths. Don't think about them."

"I'm not getting any damn implant."

"I won't either." I tried to stroke her sweaty hair.

"They're gonna force us." Her voice started to crack. "They'll force that shit in our body and we'll be controlled like everyone else."

"They can't kill us right? No death threats," I said. "How else can they force us?"

Norah's face changed in a split second from sadness to rage. "Fight."

14.

Resistance

You will be remembered in resistance.

We were walked into the city headquarters of the Intellects, a skyscraper with the words 'Equality Is Freedom' etched right above the ground floor elevators. From my knowledge it was a former corporate building functioning as both a courthouse and detention center for government agents and their captive delinquents. Norah and I were put in an interrogation room together.

Sofie Regad joined us, standing across from Norah. A smug and prim male Intellect came in after her, taking his place across from me. They sat their asses down and laid identical folders on the table. There was even a bowl of mints in the middle. I scoffed. Business in hell. Time to crack a joke.

"Isn't this the part of the movie where you take off the masks and show us your tentacles and spikes?"

The male Intellect cleared his throat in the gaping silence. "Ryan David, what is your relationship with this woman?" He gestured to Norah.

"We just met."

"Are you aware that she is a criminal?"

"I know she steals."

"It's against the law." He picked up Norah's backpack from under the table and dumped out its contents. Food, extra clothes, dog treats, and the manifesto we found in the safe.

"She steals because of you and your stupid system," I said. "All that stuff is survival."

"And this?" Sofie held up the manifesto after reading one page. "What the hell is this?"

Norah didn't look up. Didn't make a sound.

"All I see are lies about our company. Swear words and lies. Traitors against the truth."

"Damn Intellects," I said.

"If you acquire the Idlegain you will be able to buy food, a house, raise kids in one of our many approved institutions."

"We aren't married. And neither of us wants kids."

"You will." He traded smiles with Sofie Regad.

"Sir," I said, "Are you married?"

He straightened his tie. "Yes. A pleasant townhouse with one boy and three girls. And a Labrador."

I scoffed. "Who do you think you are talking to? I've been hiding from you people ever since this nightmare started. Me and Norah will fall for that peace and equality and loving the government bullshit? No flipping way."

The male Intellect folded his hands on the table. "I understand. You are resistant to change. But I have to tell you, Mr. David, your ex-wife was not."

"Ginny?"

"And you, Norah," Sofie said. She pressed a button under the table. "Do you know the name Earl Quikly?"

The door to the interrogation room opened and we saw two familiar people standing in the hallway. Ginny and Earl.

Sofie smirked at the horror on our faces. "They led us to your hiding place. They tracked you from the video store."

I closed my eyes and dropped my head before Ginny could hold my gaze. Norah was shaking so badly next to me I thought she would pass out or vomit.

"Shannon, Quikly, you may return to your duties," Sofie said. They disappeared down the hall and the door was closed.

"Now." Sofie and the male to her right opened the folders on the table. "What will it take to make you change your minds?"

"I'm not in the business of propaganda, ma'am," I said. "But I assure you I don't want any part of your brainwashed circle of life theory."

"So polite," Sofie said, smiling sweetly at me. She glanced at Norah who glared at her with a purple fury. "You've gotten away with a lot."

"My dogs," came Norah's hoarse voice.

I squirmed. I wished everyone would just keep their mouths shut.

"What about your dogs?"

"For your sake and the rest of this damn building, I need my babies."

"It's simple, hon," Sofie said. "Get the Idlegain. Then everything will go back to normal."

"Normal?" Norah huffed. She looked at me, shaking her handcuffed hands to make them rattle. "She says normal. Normal. Our lives will go back to normal, Ryan? Do you believe that?"

I didn't speak. I didn't want to waste my time debating. I was afraid to tell Norah I felt that it was over. What's the point. We're dead. That kind of pessimistic shit. But I refused to let myself say it.

Please calm down. We're fine. We're doing this together. I thought about my blossomed friendship with her. *Don't let them intimidate you, sweetheart.* And the guy in me who wanted to be more than that. *You need a hug and kiss, baby. You're freaking out too much.*

"I have a deal for you, Sofie Regad." Norah stood up, leaning over the table. "You let us go, Maguro and Sakura go, and you shove those implants up your fat ass." A mischievous smile replaced her pissed-off face.

The male Intellect and I shared a startled look. Oh shit.

Sofie straightened her jacket and flipped her hair. She grinned like a toothpaste model at her colleague. "Liam, take Mr. David to the next room. Lock the door."

15.

Ladies Only

Watch out for the 'Ladies Only' sign. They mean business.

"Where does the nerve come from, sugar? You're supposed to be one of us."

"I should ask you that. But I know the answer. You just like being top dog. Top of the pile? Queen of every damn institution. I'm supposed to agree with that, aren't I? I'm supposed to cheer and scream and jump up and down clapping like a maniac because us women finally won."

I was forced to sit in the room next door with my Intellect babysitter Mr. Troy Liam. We could hear everything being said and neither one of us wanted to admit we enjoyed a solid cat fight. We just kept our ears open and our heads down. I knew Sofie wanted to break Norah in front of me, but I doubted that either one could keep it up. They both were soap-boxing themselves hoarse.

"What do you have against me besides my place on the food chain?" Norah said.

"I wish you would just be happy that we won power."

"Power."

"Women in power." Sofie lowered her voice until I barely heard it. "You should aspire to be me."

I heard the sound of a fist slamming a table. "Aspire to be a bitch? Not on my planner this week."

"Trust me, hon," Sofie was saying, "You will be better off here."

"Do. Not. Call. Me. Honey. No one likes women as bosses. You think I'd be happy for you. I should think this is justice. The way you treat people is absolute shit. Nobody is working for you unless they are forced to."

"I can help you improve yourself."

"Improve myself?"

I heard papers shuffled over the speaker system. "You never got a degree. You never got married. Never got a credit card or rented an apartment. You never experienced men."

"Shut up."

"Oh I'm not close to finished."

"This is why I hate female Intellects." Norah's responses swung faster and sharper. In my head I had my fists raised and I chanted for a mic drop but I kept a poker face in front of Mr. Liam.

"All you do is insult me just so you feel better about yourselves. You're the same one who laughed at me for not having my nails done. You said I need a makeover to be pretty."

"Still truth. You can have a personal stylist if you joined us."

"I'd rather choke on your soy milk."

Boom. Mic drop.

My babysitter's demeanor changed and he motioned for me to stand up. "Time to regroup. Sofie's gonna slay your girl."

"Hey." I looked up at him as he adjusted my handcuffs. "Don't underestimate my girl."

"Don't underestimate her."

Mr. Liam led me back to the chamber of torture where Norah and Sofie were in a glowering contest. He knocked on the door before bringing me in and pointing to the seat next to Norah. I sat.

"Sofie, if you please, we need to do the procedure."

Sofie swiveled her head to him, nostrils flared, cheeks flushed. "Not until I make her say yes."

"That is highly unlikely. I'll be in the judge quarters when you're ready." He dipped his head at me and Norah. "We'll see you."

Norah cleared her throat. "Welcome back, Ryan. I assume you heard everything this asshole had to say."

I quickly looked at her and then at Sofie who leaned over the table, jacket open, cleavage front center.

"Yes, Ryan, did you? Your girlfriend is quite the bitch."

"I wouldn't call her that," I said.

"What?"

"Norah isn't a bitch." I pursed my lips at Sofie. "You are."

"Then you agree I'm the boss. That I have earned my power. One more thing, Norah Dean, before we force the implant in you. I have a message from your grandfather."

The room went black and a video popped up on the wall in front of us. Sofie stepped toward the door, pointing a remote at the people on screen. She wore a dirty smile.

"No shi-" Norah stopped herself. She looked wild-eyed from me to Sofie. "Where the hell? No…you didn't see this."

It was a video inside the makeshift family bunker. It looked like a regular basement except with serious military upgrades and provisions. All of Norah's family was present.

"Turn it off," I said. I looked at Norah. She was fighting tears, sniffing hard, body shuddering.

"We had cameras set up long before you all went underground." Sofie paced in front of our line of vision. "This one is from your brother's smartphone. He didn't know he was filming."

I swallowed hard. "Turn it off."

"Every traitor meets justice."

I saw one woman huddled in a corner under a blanket with a baby in her arms. She was singing a lullaby from what I could hear of the muffled audio. Another woman paced back and forth with a thick paperback in hand. She appeared to be reciting something. A grey, wispy-haired man held a thick black gun in the middle of the room. There was a calm in the picture and a warmth I had rarely seen in modern families.

"No, no, no." Norah gripped the table until her knuckles were white. She forced herself to turn away.

Gunshots entered the audio and everyone was on their feet looking at the stairway out. The explosion made me jump. Gas line. Video blackout. Everyone inside dead.

"See what guns do to innocent people? Make them insane." Sofie turned the lights back on. "They could have volunteered the implant and lived like everyone else." She picked up her folder and cordially smiled at us. "Will you be that stupid too?"

Norah bowed her head. She didn't talk back. Didn't fight.

"Time is up, Relics." Sofie reverted to all business. She pressed a button beside the door. "You're overdue for the Idlegain."

16.

Idlegain

Idlegain: A microchip for humans.

The lack of emotion, color, and sound intensified my feeling of dread. The room they called 'judge quarters' resembled a vacant hospital corridor. It was narrow and sterile. Spotless floor. At the back wall was a raised platform and leather seats where several well-dressed people observed us. A slender balcony and window were further situated above them. In the middle of the room was a glass cubicle and a grey chair prepped for torture.

"Relics," one of the judges said with a sneer. "And how terrible they look. You should have the uniform, chief," he said to me.

"I'm sorry, I don't dress like a jackass." I hinted a smile as my handcuffs were removed.

I expected Norah to pull a ninja stunt but she stayed still. I did the same, keeping my arms at my sides.

"Quite a run you've had." One of the women seated spoke. There were three men and two women. "Stealing, living underground, hoarding weapons."

"I only had one pistol," I said. "My mother gave it to me."

"You seem pretty emotional for being a thirty-nine year old man."

"I left my bravery in the interrogation room. I'm tired of running. I'm tired of being stalked and thrown under the bus by you people.

You pretend to be godsends but you're the opposite. You take dogs. You take families. You know your ideology is only meant to serve you."

"Again, chief, quite a run. Why don't you just agree that we're right and give up all that stress?"

"You're wrong." I scanned the faces of everyone in the room. "You're all wrong. About me. About Norah. About freedom. The Idlegain? It's mind control." I took one step forward. "Isn't it?"

"Allow me to explain the procedure," the same guy said, speaking as if I hadn't said a word. "It's very simple."

"I know how it's done," I said. "You shoot a chip in our arm or ear. And we become yours."

"No, chief. It takes a little longer than a standard injection to insert."

This guy enjoyed calling me 'chief' a little too much. He was younger than me for gun's sake.

"Is that because you like causing us pain, kiddo? I'm old enough to be your dad I think. How about a little more respect for the geezer?"

Junior Judge pointed a gloved finger at us. "Relics don't belong in this society. You and your quiet little girlfriend need to straighten up."

"Okay, Junior. I'll make you a deal. You let us run free and shoot our backs. We'd rather die anyway."

Norah jerked her head up and looked from me to them.

Junior Judge chuckled, rising to his feet. "Please, Relic, refer to me as Mr. Lingen. And you know our policy on arms by now.

Banned." He fumed at us, stomping like a bull on speed. "All weapons banned!"

His scream echoed in the room. I saw everyone's eyes following the sound and then his harsh breathing. Enraged Intellect. Not pretty.

"Mr. Lingen." I spread my hands. "You gotta give respect to get it. Even to the likes of us."

"You." He spat as he talked. "Are a damn plague."

"Sir," one of the women said, "Call in the doctor." She tried to get Junior's attention. "Sit down."

Junior refused to return to his cushy throne. He wagged his head, cackling like a maniac as he went down the stairs toward me and Norah.

"Let me tell you about your future. You get everything you don't deserve. You can work here with me if you like. Once the implant is inserted, ten seconds after, you will be reborn into our family."

Psycho. Psycho. Shit. Shit. Shit. My mind pounded out every fear and insult. The adrenaline this guy was promoting…I knew Norah wasn't taking it well. But she was as stone-faced as I'd seen her.

"The pros of the Intellect," he said in an extra theatrical voice. He read off an index card, pacing in front of us with one arm behind his back. "A form of payment for whatever your need or desire. A means of reading people before you meet them. A sense of security, knowing the government always has your back. And feeling equal with every one of your neighbors. No more envy. No more coveting fashionable shoes or the latest haircut. You get it all with the Idlegain."

"Cons?" I asked.

He grinned and tucked the card into the inside pocket of his jacket. "There are none."

On one hand I considered the vast majority of Intellects to be piss and vinegar goofballs. On the other...they were true threats to our former way of life. This guy. This guy calling himself "Mr. Lingen" was a real cartoon character. He had long blond hair that looked like he was advertising as an Elf and an evil scientist in the same show.

"You two are disgusting. Covered in sand and dog hair. We find you cowering at a beach in an arcade with no power. Why? It's ludicrous."

"Why don't you do something about the public toilets?" I asked him. "I poked my head in one of those and about pissed in my shorts. That's ludicrous."

Junior smirked, walking back and forth. I couldn't take the waiting. The silence.

"When did you get the Idlegain?"

"Four months ago." He winked and raised a hand to my cheek which I smacked away. "And I love it." He slapped me across the face. Then slapped Norah.

"Sonofabitch." Norah sprang out of her coma, swinging her fists to pound him.

"Restrain them," he said too calmly.

I counted five seconds before my arms were yanked behind my back by a bouncer-built security guard. Norah was restrained by Junior and walked into the glass cubicle.

"Sit still unless you want to be hit again, darling."

The guard kicked the back of my legs to force me on my knees. I fought until he moved his forearm across my throat. "Relax, Relic. She goes first."

"Don't…do this to her," I managed to strain out my mouth.

Junior pet Norah's hair with a childish gleam. "The doctor is on his way in. I'd give you the Idlegain myself, darling, but I'm not qualified to work with needles."

I saw Norah trying to control her anger. She closed her eyes as the young judge teased her with strokes on her head and chest. At the present moment I resigned myself that we were both screwed as far as freedom. We never expect good memories to come in the end, but that's exactly what came to my mind. Strange but comforting.

I remembered the night I held my niece for the first time, the lullaby that I made up when she started crying, how I cradled her in the pink blanket and bobbed around my sister's hospital room like a kayak on morning wakes. Real life was nothing like that moment. Nothing was calmer than that night holding my newborn niece. Time stopped for me as it did for little Glory.

Why did I recall this memory moments before I would be given the Idlegain? I don't know. I can't tell you. But it fogged up the real world. It turned all the humans in the room to vapor. I was alone.

"Hi, baby girl. Hi, Glory. I'm your Uncle Ryan." I sang some doofy song about penguins and ice cream. She whimpered in her blanket. I sang some more. The sky was dark outside the window. My sister was in the bathroom. I had my little niece to myself. Afraid to drop her. Afraid to let her go. But I rocked. I sang. I talked to her. "It's okay. This place is big huh? Big and bright and cool. When you get older I'm gonna build you a dollhouse and little furniture. I'll make you smile." Her eyes opened and I stared into those itsy blue ponds. "Hi, baby girl. I got you."

"Ryan David."

"Norah Dean."

Our names were announced separately before the door opened. The medical professional approached, his polished dress shoes clacking on the incandescent floor.

"You are long overdue." He joined Norah in the cubicle and motioned Junior to step out. He quickly sifted around before holding up a syringe from within a small drawer. Norah's chin quivered when he lifted her head to look in his eyes. "Now, my dear, where do you want it?"

"Norah! Kick the bastard!" My voice echoed. It rang in my own ears.

The action in the room suddenly paused. All eyes drifted to the balcony above the judges. A shadowed person leaned against the wall there, waiting. The realization hit three seconds too late for the Intellects.

"He's got a gun!"

Every one of them left their post, doctor included. The cereal box superhero in me dove toward Norah and knocked her flat inside the cubicle. I laid on top of her, my hands pressed to her head. Several rounds danced around before there was the kind of silence that made you taste acid at the back of your throat. The shooter was standing above us.

I looked up. No one.

"Where is he?" I asked myself.

Norah crept out of the cubicle that had shattered. The doctor was dead. Two of the judges were dead. Junior had managed to escape.

"Norah," I whispered. "Let's go. Come on, let's go."

She sat on the floor. "What about my dogs? Sakura. Maguro. Let's find my dogs."

"They're gonna get us. We have to leave. We have to get out of this building now, Norah."

"Fine." She snarled and scrambled up. "Back to the arcade."

"No." I grabbed her arm. "Listen to me. There's a better place. I know you're angry. I know you're tired. You have to trust me. Please, baby girl." I flinched as I misspoke. "You have to trust me."

She nodded and headed for the emergency exit that was on the same side as the balcony. I spun around, viewing the corpses, wondering where the shooter was, who they were. My back was turned when I heard the alarm ring through the building.

We ran.

17.

Home

There is nothing like going home.

My plan was to lay low in a former childhood hangout. The attic of the Wilber Hotel. We stole bikes down an alley and rode toward the beach, this time making a detour in my very first hideout. The sewers.

"Sorry it's not stocked with imported wine and cheese. I'll have to hire a butler when we get to the hotel." I looked back to see if Norah was smiling at my joke. She wasn't.

"Not a wine person?"

"This place is disgusting. Can't even breathe without inhaling snot in here."

"Hey. They would've inserted that shit into both of us. Whoever had that gun did us a favor."

"I know that. Now they're on a hunt for three Relics."

"Technically," I said, "There are hundreds of us left. Maybe thousands. All underground. But if any have shelters like your family, they better have their damn phones off."

"Asshole." Norah pushed me against a slimy wall. "My brother's phone had nothing to do with their deaths."

"You told me it was suicide."

"No. Murder. That bitch said it all. She admitted her sins."

"Sofie Regad admitted to nothing. You gotta forget them."

Norah became emotional, grinding her teeth and blinking her eyes fiercely. "I don't want to forget. That was my house. My home I came back to every day until they told me to leave. They got to die together. I have nothing!" She made a fist and raised it before collapsing against me. "I wanna go home."

I held her with my own heightened emotion. "You knew you couldn't run forever."

We just delay the inevitable.

She backed away from me. I studied her tear-stained face, her frazzled red hair, her childish t-shirt and shorts on bruised legs. "You're a soldier," I said. I took her hand in mine and kept walking through the sewers. We had nothing to carry. No belongings. No survival gear.

"This hotel," Norah asked me. "Why didn't they tear it down?"

"They left it for the insects and other wild things. I think it was the peace-loving bunch who claimed the place as sacred land."

"The Intellects believed that?"

"No, but they didn't want to upset the nests of spiders and rats there."

"Mm," Norah said. "Comforting." She walked closer to me, linking her arm to mine. "I don't mind spiders. I talk to them."

I laughed. "You would. I used to talk to my cat and copy his weird stretches to make my niece spray milk out her nose."

I heard Norah chuckle. "You loved being an uncle?"

"Yeah. I would still be except my sister was right there in the city when the implant hype started. She made sure her daughter got it. My family's kinda splintered but I know they all lined up for the Idlegain."

"You were the rebel?"

"Yeah. Yeah, I was. That's why I clicked with Ginny at first. She didn't follow rules. She was a wild girl."

"Until the Idlegain. Boy, she must have gone after that thing like a supermodel after rice cakes."

"Pretty much. A bit of an airhead."

Norah smiled. "You're too smart for an airhead, Ryan. And you're too attractive at your age to have given up."

I looked at her. "I'd just as quickly take you out to a movie as I would have with Ginny."

She shrugged. "Then do it."

"What?"

"Take me to a movie."

I couldn't hide my smile. "I am."

Norah's eyebrows scrunched. "Where?" She pointed at the ladder to exit the sewer. "Out there?"

I continued to smile. I leaned in to kiss her cheek. "Idlegain-free."

18.

Guard

Respect the old guard.

I lost track of time almost every day after I started living underground. When I did have the pleasure of seeing a sunrise or sunset, it was like the world was at peace with itself and humanity on its surface. Sunsets got me the most. I hated watching the sun disappear. The night was a lonely place.

"Is this it?"

The abandoned hotel was several miles adjacent to the coastline. From the top of the building, in the attic, you could see a giant video screen planted at a public park. It never mattered what movie was playing. For Relics who could see it from a distance, it reminded us of what normal used to mean.

Norah and I had made the walk up the over hundred steps to get to the attic and she leaned out the tiny window. It was stuffy and hot. We had to keep our distance from that window to avoid being caught by Intellect cameras.

"Limit your time there," I said. "I know you need air but they got spies all over."

"Just watching the movie."

I let her be as I searched the stack of storage boxes. "Are you a cereal eater?"

"A what?"

I shook the box of sugar flakes that was in my hand. "My stash. Still here."

Norah moved back from the window, sitting against a dusty bookshelf. "Bummer there's no milk."

I passed another cereal box to her. This one had remnants of chocolate shapes at the bottom of the plastic bag. "After my divorce I would eat three bowls from midnight. Every night. Had the TV on. Usually some survival nature show."

"I lived your nature shows. I practiced starting fires and chopping wood all the time."

"Did you really like that lifestyle?"

"I got tired sometimes, but the boys in my family were competition. I wanted to keep up."

We crunched in silence for several minutes, enjoying the flavors of our cereal. I liked that Norah was willing to try anything to stay alive. I admired her risks and the love she had for her family.

"I gotta be honest," I said. "I lied in the interrogation room about not wanting kids."

"Why?"

"I don't know. But I did imagine succeeding in the old school American dream."

Norah chuckled as she munched her chocolate shapes. "Giving up on world domination, Ryan?"

"I never wanted that."

"You want a wife and kids. That's called world domination."

I leaned into a corner of the attic, folding my arms. "How's that?"

"My definition of world domination is a dream come true. That's your dream."

"Well." I looked at a spider sitting on a web. "Dreams don't ever work."

"Stars work. They dominate the sky without any effort."

"What?" I raised an eyebrow. "We speaking philosophical shit?"

Norah crawled forward, looking through the mess of boxes on the floor. Sweat kept her shirt stuck to her chest. "I mean that I wish I had gotten a degree in astronomy."

I watched her crawl around, pulling my knee up to make more room. "And what would you do with astronomy?"

She smiled, lifting her eyes to mine. She spoke in a coy whisper. "You never had the urge to blast off away from all these conceited assholes on Earth?"

I smirked. "Just off myself. Less training involved."

"I'm tired," Norah muttered.

"You can sleep. It's safe here."

She plopped next to me and laid her head on my shoulder. "You sure they aren't gonna send a dozen rockets screaming at us?"

I put my arm around her. "Yeah, I'm sure."

"What's that?" She pointed to a plaque on the opposite wall.

I squinted to read it. "The old guard. It's an antique I think. Another Relic put it up here. We are the old guard. Keepers of history. Kind of romantic."

"Especially if we die," Norah muttered into my shoulder.

"Psh. Aren't you optimistic."

"Optimistic as a sheep in the slaughter line. Stupid as can be."

Old guard, I thought. *Wouldn't it be fantastic to have that on my tombstone? We are the old guard. Keepers of history. The old guard.*

"Old guard," I whispered.

I don't know what time it was but eventually we fell asleep. Sweaty, bruised, and emotionally dead.

19.

Courage

The last moment of freedom is courage.

It was still dark outside when Norah and I struggled to come out of sleep. I found a water jug I had hid in the attic some months ago and we took turns drinking. The only entertainment was to talk.

"Remember when we thought computers were cool?"

She smiled, red hair falling in her eyes. "Yeah. First time I used one was at a library. I forgot what I looked up online but I remember typing with two fingers and watching the cursor blink. I was naive for a long time about technology. Parents protected me."

"I remember when computers were big and boxy machines. They got smaller and smaller. And videos. I had a DVD collection. Hundreds."

"What kind of movies?"

"Stuff from the 80s. A lot of indie films. What did you watch?"

"Didn't watch movies. Not until I was like eighteen."

"You had a weird childhood," I said.

"It was fine. I used my imagination unlike everyone else my age."

"What did you imagine?"

"That I was a pirate princess hiding in the woods. I built my own secret fort. Rope swing too."

I poured water into my hand and ran it through my hair. "What else did you build?"

"I helped make a stable once. I've repaired a roof. My hands aren't as rough as they should be. I always wore gloves."

"Do you know how interesting you are?" I said.

"Just a Relic."

"So am I. Worth nothing in this world right?"

"Worth something once." She faced me. "Did you like music?"

"Of course. I could dance to anything. I had a little cassette player that ran on batteries. My mom gave it to me a long time ago."

Norah held the water jug in her lap. "So Relic."

I rummaged through the cardboard box next to me. There were traces of rat crap and spider webs all over everything. And then I saw it.

"Shit, Norah. Look."

She stared at what I held.

"It's a cassette player." I checked the battery compartment and saw that they were clean and fully intact.

"Who would've left that here?" she asked.

I didn't answer. I didn't see a label on the tape that was inside. So I pressed down PLAY.

Real rock. Real guitar strums. Familiar drum patterns. I couldn't remember a name or who sang. All it reminded me of was how it used to be. The music my parents played on the stereo from their days. Slightly crackly but so real. No auto-tune. No layers. Just pure, sweet rock and roll. Lyrics we could all understand. No hidden agendas. Just a talented group of musicians telling their story the way they wanted it told.

"My parents," Norah said. "They had music like this."

I held my hand out. "C'mon."

Given the situation, dancing was a ridiculous pursuit. But time was limited. So was freedom. I spun Norah around and showed her my air guitar.

"Old school chill," I said. "When 'cool' meant something different."

The sound from the cassette player was very crackly. But it still emitted a danceable tune. We were sweaty from the heat of the attic as we traded awful dance moves. For the first time there was a real smile on Norah's face. I took her hands and swayed with her as the music switched to an acoustic guitar-focused ballad. I was reminded of my first prom dance. The awkward parts.

"I'm sorry I don't do elegant dancing well."

"It's okay." She looked in my eyes. "We're just swaying."

In the middle of our slow dance I could hear rustling outside the window. We had covered it with a sheet. I knew who it was. I didn't stop moving with Norah. *Images of circling helicopters and Sofie Regad climbing stairs with a bullhorn and tranquilizer gun. We are surrounded. We are no longer free.*

I wanted to pretend it was okay. For Norah. For Maguro and Sakura. For every Relic still on the run. I wanted to pretend that we would take back society. We would win the war for justice.

"Ryan, I'd rather die."

"I know."

"What if we jumped?" she said against my shoulder.

"The building's not high enough," I said.

Agents charging up the stairs. Windows busted. Led by a psychotic Intellect.

"You said they wouldn't touch this building."

"We changed that rule," I said.

We hugged each other. Heads down.

20.

Relic

Everyone will become a Relic.

Humans try to predict their futures. They try to predict their deaths. But in the end we all fail to acknowledge one truth. We are not in control.

Hear me out.

One way or another this world will be destroyed to make way for a new one. A utopia perhaps. But not under the reign of the Intellects. We sabotage ourselves with hatred and anger and violence while holding up signs of love. We claim freedom and peace for all society. We say that new is better. That technology is the hope of the world.

Who are we trying to fool? We are all weapons to society. To each other. To happiness. To equality. To freedom. We could turn it around and make something beautiful but no one wants to agree with each other. No one wants to preserve the old guard or give old school policies another shot. Truth? The cycle will move and break itself. And move and break itself. And break itself. Over and over and over. Until we pay attention to the final outcome.

Decades down the road there will be more conflict and a loss of empathy toward nostalgia and history. Respect for Relics is near nonexistent. The new society silences anything past its due, and they will make it extinct by their own law. We can run for weeks and months, but they will catch up. We can try to hide in sturdy bunkers, but they will survey us through our phones.

We all become Relics.

We are our own downfall.

As every solid movie villain has said in their own words, "Sit back and watch the fireworks."

They're coming.

21.

The End

I rat her die than b part of sys tem.

Sometimes life is messy. It won't make sense. Like my view of the world. My story. It won't make sense to everyone. But it matters. We matter. Relics.

I warned you.

About The Author

Mattie J. Garby is an old soul who loves singing country in the car and frolicking with her dogs, iced coffee in hand. She is a minimalist with words and a lover of all animals. Half her heart is in the ocean while the other is in the mountains. The west coast beaches are her great escape.